W9-DDK-137

One Wonderful
Fine Day for a
Sculpin Named Sam

WRITTEN BY
AL PITTMAN

ILLUSTRATED BY
SHAWN O'HAGAN

One Wonderful Fine Day for a Sculpin Named Sam

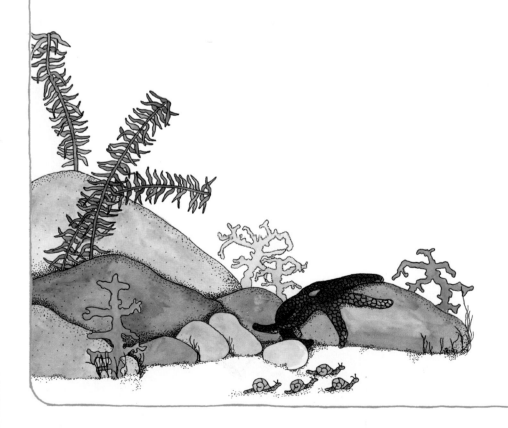

1 Stamp's Lane, St. John's, NL, Canada, A1E 3C9

www.breakwaterbooks.com

Copyright © 1983 Breakwater Books Ltd.
ISBN 0-919948-86-3
Copyright © 2013 Breakwater Books Ltd.
ISBN 978-0-919948-86-0

Library and Archives Canada Cataloguing in Publication
Pittman, Al, 1940-2001
One wonderful fine day for a sculpin named Sam /
by Al Pittman ; illustrated by Shawn O'Hagan.
ISBN 978-0-919948-86-0
I. O'Hagan, Shawn, 1950- II. Title.
PS8531.I86O54 2013   jC813'.54   C2012-907678-3

All Rights Reserved. No part of this publication may be reproduced, stored in
a retrieval system or transmitted, in any form or by any means, without
the prior written consent of the publisher or a licence from The Canadian
Copyright Licensing Agency (Access Copyright). For an Access Copyright licence,
visit www.accesscopyright.ca or call toll free to 1-800-893-5777.

We acknowledge the support of the Canada Council for the Arts, which last year
invested $154 million to bring the arts to Canadians throughout the
country. We acknowledge the Government of Canada through the Canada Book Fund
and the Government of Newfoundland and Labrador through the Department of
Tourism, Culture and Recreation for our publishing activities.

Breakwater Books is committed to choosing papers and materials
for our books that help to protect our environment. To this end,
this book is printed on a recycled paper that is certified by the
Forest Stewardship Council®.

Printed in India

THIS BOOK IS FOR

Kyran, Emily, Edith, Alban, Jonathan, Rebecca, Karina,
Darius, and the children of Fogo Island. It is also for
all children everywhere, and especially for Dennis Lee.

THIS ANNIVERSARY EDITION IS DEDICATED TO
a new generation of young readers
and especially to our grandchildren:
Alden, Jonah, and Carey
Remy and Maida Leigh
Eamon, Lucy, Finn, and Levi

 **ONCE**, just a little while ago and just off the northeast coast of Newfoundland, there lived a sculpin named Sam.

Sam's home was under a fishing stage in a harbour on an island called Fogo.

Sam lived all alone but he had lots of neighbours because lots of other fish lived nearby.

One warm summer day when the sun was shining all the way down to the bottom of the harbour, Sam thought he'd take a little flick around to see what was going on.

He had no sooner left the shadow of the stage when he came upon Tom Conner swimming busily about.

"A fine day like this," thought Sam, "I suppose he's out looking for someone to do a little work around his rock."

Whenever Tom decided he wanted to trim the seaweed in his garden, or enlarge the room beneath his rock, or get rid of stuff brought into his yard by the tide, he'd call on his neighbours and they'd come eagerly to help him out.

"I don't imagine he'll invite me to help," thought Sam, "but you never know."

"Wonderful fine day!" said Sam to Tom.

"Wonderful!" said Tom, looking the other way. And with a quick flick of his tail, he shot right past Sam as fast as he could go.

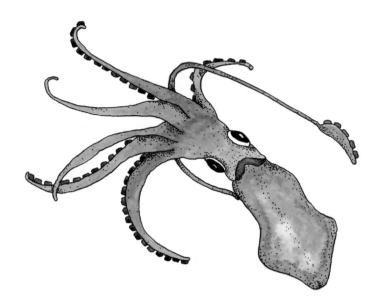

"Oh well!" thought Sam, as he watched Tom stop to talk with Sid Squid a short distance away.

"I wish the lord-liftin'-lumpfish he'd just up and shift," Sam heard Tom say.

"Yeah!" snarled Sid. "We could do without the likes of that around here."

"Who would they be talking about now?" wondered Sam as he watched them swim off together.

When they were out of sight, Sam glided around a corner of the stage and came upon Lemuel Lumpfish and Jeremiah Jellyfish loitering there as usual.

"Wonderful fine day!" said Sam to both, thinking he might stop and have a little chat.

"Lem, you going over to Larry Lobster's for a game of shells this afternoon?" asked Jeremiah, ignoring Sam entirely.

"I'm not much of a hand at shells," replied Lemuel, "but I dare say I'll drop by."

"The rest of the crowd will be there," said Jeremiah. "It'll be a fine time."

"See you later then!" said Lemuel. And off they went in different directions without ever so much as a glance at Sam.

"A game of shells! That'd be some fun," thought Sam. "But it'd be a frozen Friday indeed before they'd ever let me be in on anything like that."

Feeling quite left out of everything, Sam decided he'd be better off if he avoided meeting anyone else. So he headed back into the shadows beneath the stage.

"They'll all be out in the sun today," he thought. "Better for me to be in the dark by myself."

Alas! He'd no sooner reached the shade of the stage when he swam smack into Ella Eel and Lila Lobster.

Ella and Lila had been so absorbed in their aches and pains and so busy complaining to each other about the sunlight outside, that neither of them noticed Sam until they were staring him in the face.

"Do you mind!" they spat at Sam together. And if looks could kill, Sam would have keeled over on the spot.

"Wonderful fine day!" stammered Sam as he backed away embarrassed.

Ella and Lila stopped talking until Sam was almost out of hearing. Then they went at it in very loud whispers.

"Yuk!" said Ella.

"Gives me the willies!" said Lila.

"There ought to be a law!" said Ella.

"Absolutely!" said Lila.

"Enough to make you sick!" whispered both as loud as they could.

"I wonder what's got their dander up," thought Sam deciding now that he might be better off on the bottom of the harbour.

"Some wonderful fine day, no mistake!" muttered Sam as he let himself sink.

Lo and behold! No sooner had his belly touched bottom when the bottom exploded, leaving Sam as blind as a batfish in a cloud of mud.

He hadn't noticed Freeman Flatfish lying there sound asleep. And no wonder! It's almost impossible to tell the difference between flatfish and anything else that might be tucked into the mud on the bottom of the sea.

"Stupid sculpin!" snarled Freeman, settling down in the mud again.

"Sorry, Freeman!" sputtered Sam.

"Sorry?" snorted Freeman. "I suppose you are. For a minute there I thought I was having a nightmare."

And with that, Freeman closed his lop-sided eyes and went back to sleep.

Sam tried to think where in the whole harbour he could go and not be a bother to anyone else. But before he could figure out where that might be, he decided he wanted to know, once and for all, why the other fish treated him the way they did.

"As far as I know," he said to himself, "I've never done any harm to anyone here and still all I ever get are insults and hard looks. What is it they've got against me anyway? That's what I'd like to know."

And then, just before he was about to swim away, he said to himself, "It's high time I found out!"

And with all the gumption he could gather, he nudged Freeman out of his sleep.

"Not again!" moaned Freeman, who hated waking up more than anything else in the world.

"It's me!" said Sam, trying to sound oh so much braver than he really felt.

"I could tell that, even with my eyes closed," grumbled Freeman. "What the devilfish do you want now?"

"I want to know," said Sam, "why everyone around here is so friendly to everyone else and so snarky to me."

"Oh!" said Freeman, almost surprised.

"Yes!" said Sam. "I've lived in this harbour a long time now and no one has ever allowed me so much as the time of day. And I'd like to know how come?"

"You would, would you?" asked Freeman firmly.

"Yes!" said Sam uncertainly. "I certainly would."

"If you could see yourself," said Freeman, "you wouldn't have to ask such a stupid question."

"What do you mean by that?" asked Sam.

"Holy mackerel!" declared Freeman. "Just look at the bulges you got for eyes! And all those splotchy blotches all over you! Looks like a rash if you ask me! And all those boney bumps and lumps! And that head for Heaven's sake! What kind of mixed up mess is that to have for a head?"

"I don't know!" said Sam, baffled.

"Don't you know what that makes you?" moaned Freeman, wondering how, on top of everything else, sculpins could be so stupid.

"No!" said Sam. "What?"

"It makes you ugly!" said Freeman. "That's what!"

"Ugly?" said Sam.

"Ugly!" blared Freeman. "Ugly! Ugly! Ugly!"

"Oh!" said Sam.

"Guaranteed!" said Freeman. And he snuggled down in the mud again to get on with his nap.

"So!" thought Sam sadly. "That explains that."

And as he turned to examine what little he could see of himself, he realized for the first time why all the other fish wanted to be rid of him.

"Can't say I blame them either!" he sobbed. "With all these splotches and blotches and bumps and lumps, I imagine I'm quite the sight to see."

Sam wondered then why he had ever been born.

"How come I wasn't born to be a whale?" he thought. "Or a wolf fish, or a dogfish, or even a foolish clam? Why, of all the creatures in the sea, did I have to be born an ugly old sculpin?"

And he wondered if there was anywhere in all the oceans on earth where he could live out of sight and be satisfied.

"Not likely!" thought Sam as he swam off due North, all sorrow and sadness, going nowhere.

He was half way out the Eastern Tickle that led from the harbour into the vast Atlantic, when, to his surprise, he heard someone call his name.

"Sammy!" a strange voice called behind him.

For a moment Sam thought some of the youngster fish had come to call him names and make fun of him.

"Sammy! Sammy Sculpin!" the voice called again.

And suddenly Sam realized that he hadn't heard anyone call him "Sammy" since he'd been a youngster fish himself.

Not knowing what to expect, but expecting the worst all the same, Sam turned around.

And there, swimming toward him, was the most beautiful fish he'd ever seen in his entire life.

"Hi!" said the beautiful fish.

Sam wished he could disappear.

"I bet you don't even remember me," said the beautiful fish. "I'm Sara."

"Sara?" stammered Sam.

"Sara Sculpin," said Sara. "Remember?"

Sam was flabbergasted. Sam hadn't seen Sara since his childhood. And now, suddenly, here she was, all grown up and prettier than he had ever imagined any fish could be.

"Jumpin's!" said Sam.

"It's been years," said Sara.

"Jumpin's!" said Sam, again, wishing he could get his tongue untied.

Sam had never seen such beautiful bulging eyes, or such beautiful blotchy splotches, or such beautiful bumpy lumps, or such a beautiful horny head. And he had never ever felt the strange tingling way he felt now, suddenly, inside.

The more he looked at Sara, the more Sam despised his own ugliness. And the more he thought about it, the more he wanted to turn and swim away from her forever.

"Remember," said Sara, "when we used to play hide-n-seek around that old wreck?"

"Yes!" said Sam sadly. "I remember."

And then it dawned on Sam that Sara wasn't ignoring him or being nasty to him. In fact she seemed rather friendly.

Sam didn't know what to make of it.

"I used to think you were so cute," said Sara.

"Oh, oh!" thought Sam. "Here it comes!"

"You were too," said Sara blinking her big eyes. "You were a very handsome young fish."

"Handsome?" stammered Sam. "Me?"

"Oh, yes!" gurgled Sara. "You certainly were."

"Then I must have changed a lot," said Sam.

"Not at all," said Sara, "except you've grown up."

"I've grown up to be ugly!" said Sam, and immediately turned to swim away.

"Ugly?" said Sara. "You're not ugly."

"I'm not?" said Sam, turning back with disbelief written all over his face.

"Not at all," said Sara. "Where in Neptune's name did you ever get such a silly notion?"

"Well, everyone else…," Sam began.

"To tell the truth," said Sara waving her tail back and forth just so, "I think you're still very handsome."

"You do?" stammered Sam.

"Yes I do!" said Sara.

"Cross your heart?" asked Sam anxiously.

"Cross my heart!" said Sara, twinkling all over.

Suddenly Sam felt as though a wave had washed all his ugliness away. He felt he could leap into the sky like dolphins do or sail away on the wind like a gull.

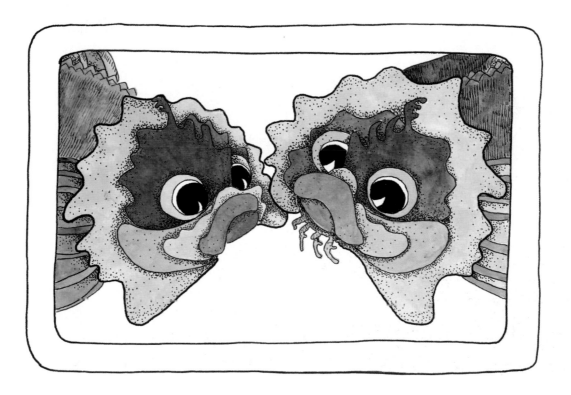

"I bet you don't remember the name
of that old schooner," said Sam playfully.
"I give up," said Sara.

"The Northern Star!" said Sam. And then he added, wishing
with all his might, "Would you like to see it again?"
"I'd love to!" said Sara.

"Come on then," said
Sam smiling handsomely.
"I'll lead the way."

And together, Sam and Sara swam back into the harbour, heading happily toward The Northern Star.

Half way there they met Tom Conner who was on his way to Larry Lobster's to play shells.

"Wonderful fine day!" said Sam to Tom. And for the first time in a long, long time, he really meant it.

"Sculpins!" spat Tom as he darted away. "I don't see how they can stand one another."

Sam paid no attention. He was too happily enthralled watching Sara's sunlit fins waving gently as she swam along close by his side.

AS it turned out, it was indeed a wonderful fine day for Sam Sculpin. And though he could not have known so at the time, it was just the first of many such days he was to share (and still does share, somewhere down by Fogo) with Sara, his bridefish, his beloved.

One of Newfoundland's most celebrated writers, **AL PITTMAN** was a prolific author of poetry, drama, songs, and children's literature, and the winner of numerous literary awards. His perennial children's classics include *Down by Jim Long's Stage*, *One Wonderful Fine Day for a Sculpin Named Sam*, and *On a Wing and a Wish: Salt Water Bird Rhymes*. A longtime resident of Corner Brook, NL, Pittman passed away in 2001, at the age of sixty-one.

SHAWN O'HAGAN was born in Toronto and has made her home in Newfoundland. She has illustrated seven children's books including *Flights of Magic* by John Steffler, which was nominated for a Governor General's Award for Children's Book Illustration, and Robert Munch's *Get Me Another One*.